A Note to Parents and Caregivers:

Read-it! Joke Books are for children who are moving ahead on the amazing road to reading. These fun books support the acquisition and extension of reading skills as well as a love of books.

Published by the same company that produces *Read-it!* Readers, these books introduce the question/answer and dialogue patterns that help children expand their thinking about language structure and book formats.

When sharing joke books with a child, read in short stretches. Pause often to talk about the pictures and the meaning of the jokes. The question/answer and dialogue formats work well for this purpose. Have the child turn the pages and point to the pictures and familiar words. When you read the jokes, have fun creating the voices of characters or emphasizing some important words. And be sure to reread favorite jokes.

There is no right or wrong way to share books with children. Find time to read with your child, and pass on the legacy of literacy.

Adria F. Klein, Ph.D.
Professor Emeritus
California State University
San Bernardino, California

Managing Editor: Bob Temple
Creative Director: Terri Foley
Editor: Peggy Henrikson
Editorial Adviser: Andrea Cascardi
Designer: Amy Muehlenhardt
Page production: Picture Window Books
The illustrations in this book were prepared digitally.

Picture Window Books
5115 Excelsior Boulevard
Suite 232
Minneapolis, MN 55416
1-877-845-8392
www.picturewindowbooks.com

Copyright © 2004 by Picture Window Books
All rights reserved. No part of this book may be reproduced without written
permission from the publisher. The publisher takes no responsibility for the
use of any of the materials or methods described in this book, nor for the
products thereof.

Printed in the United States of America.

Library of Congress Cataloging-in-Publication Data
Dahl, Michael.
Under arrest! : a book of police jokes / written by Michael Dahl ;
illustrated by Brian Jensen.
p. cm. — (Read-it! joke books)
Summary: A collection of jokes and riddles about police, including,
"What do you call a flying police officer? A helicopper."
ISBN 1-4048-0306-8
1. Police—Juvenile humor. 2. Wit and humor, Juvenile. [1. Police—
Wit and Humor. 2. Jokes. 3. Riddles] I. Jensen, Brian, ill. II. Title.
PN6231.P59 D34 2004
818'.5402—dc22

2003016665

MAR 2 4 2004

EAST HAMPTON LIBRARY

Under Arrest

A Book of Police Jokes

Read-it! Joke Books
Green Level

Michael Dahl • Illustrated by Brian Jensen

Reading Advisers:
Adria F. Klein, Ph.D.
Professor Emeritus, California State University
San Bernardino, California

Susan Kesselring, M.A., Literacy Educator
Rosemount-Apple Valley-Eagan (Minnesota) School District

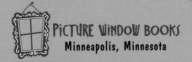

PICTURE WINDOW BOOKS
Minneapolis, Minnesota

What do you call a flying police officer?

Police

A helicopper.

5

What did the thief say when he robbed the glue factory?

"This is a stickup!"

What do you call a freezing police officer?

A copsicle.

Officer: "I thought I told you to take those penguins to the zoo!"
Tom: "I did. We had such a good time that today I'm taking them to the beach!" 9

What did the picture say when the cop sent it to jail by mistake?

"I've been framed!"

Officer: "Call your dog! He's chasing a man on a bicycle."

Dog owner: "That must be somebody else's dog. Mine can't ride a bicycle." 11

What is a robber's favorite dinner?

cafe

Takeout.

What do traffic cops have in their sandwiches?

Traffic jam.

Why was the bird arrested by the police?

Because it was a-robbin'. 15

Why did the police look inside the cement mixer?

They were looking for
hardened criminals.

Why did the police officer arrest the kittens?

Because of the kitty litter.

What kind of robber has the strongest arms?

A shoplifter.

Why did the police officer arrest the suspenders?

Because they held up
a pair of pants.

Officer: "That's a funny
place to wear it!"   23

Why did the burglar take a shower?

He wanted to make
a clean getaway.

EAST HAMPTON LIBRARY

3 0625 00077 9593

jE   Dahl, Michael
DAHL
            Under arrest

East Hampton Library
159 Main St.
East Hampton, NY 11937

GAYLORD M